DIGGING UP THE PAST

The SEARCH for DINOSAURS

DOUGAL DIXON

Thomson Learning • New York

DIGGING UP THE PAST
Biblical Sites • Bodies from the Past • Pompeii and Herculaneum • The Search for Dinosaurs • Troy and Knossos • The Valley of the Kings

Cover background: A scene of herding hadrosaurs.

Cover inset: The horns of a *Triceratops* were ideal weapons to fight off other meat-eating dinosaurs.

Title page: The fate of the dinosaurs—extinction.

Consultant: Dr. Michael J. Benton, Reader in Vertebrate Palaeontology, University of Bristol, England.

First published in the United States in 1995 by Thomson Learning New York, NY

Published simultaneously in Great Britain by Wayland (Publishers) Ltd.

Library of Congress Cataloging in Publication Data

Dixon, Dougal.
  The search for dinosaurs / Dougal Dixon.
       p.   cm. (Digging up the past)
  Includes bibliographic references (p.   ) and index.
  ISBN 1-56847-396-6 (hc)
  1. Dinosaurs—Juvenile literature. [1. Dinosaurs.
2. Paleontology.] I. Title. II. Series: Digging up the past
(New York, N.Y.)
QE862.D5D556 1995
567.9'1—dc20   94-14685

Printed in Italy

Picture acknowledgments
The publishers would like to thank the following for allowing their photographs to be reproduced in this book: American Museum of Natural History, New York 23 (Neg. No. 17808/Osborn & Brown), 40 (Neg. No. 324393 / R. T. Bird). Courtesy of the Department of Library Services, American Museum of Natural History; Bruce Coleman Ltd. 22 (J. Burton); Mary Evans Picture Library 8, 11, 35; Natural History Museum, London *cover* (both), 4, 6 , 7, 9 (J. Sibbick), 10 (bottom), 19, 20, 21, 31, 32, 39; Oxford Scientific Films 5 (F. Gohier), 14 (B. P. Kent), 24 (R. T. Nowitz), 28 (J. L. Amos), 36 (B. P. Kent), 37 (J. L. Amos), 38 top (E. R. Degginer), 38 bottom (J. Kaprielian), 41 (M. Birkhead); Peabody Museum 17 bottom and 18 (Courtesy of the Peabody Museum of Natural History, Yale University); Royal Tyrrell Museum, Alberta, Canada 25 (C. Orthner); Science Photo Library 42.
The original artwork on pages 12–13, 15, 27, 30, 34 and 43 is by Luis Rey. The maps on pages 18, 26, and 29 are by Peter Bull.

Contents

Searching for a Giant—
Tyrannosaurus Rex

In 1902, a piece of fossil bone lay as a paperweight on the desk of William Hornaday, the director of the New York Zoological Society. That was the beginning. Barnum Brown, a fossil collector and discoverer of dinosaurs, recognized it for what it was—a piece of *Triceratops* horn.

Brown looked at photographs of the area in Montana where Hornaday had found the horn while out hunting. He recognized the landscape as good "dinosaur country," and was off! A train to Miles City, Montana, then a five-day trek by a hired wagon brought Brown to the handful of log cabins that made up the town of Jordan. There he began exploring the rocks of the dramatically named Hell Creek Formation.

Brown came to the ranch where Hornaday had picked up his horn. Almost as soon as Brown pitched camp he saw embedded fossil bones—noticeable in the evening light by their dark-brown color against the blue of the flinty sandstone. Brown and his workers realized they were staring at the remains of something that had never been seen before. He left them in place and dug out some other dinosaur skeletons, which were easier to take out.

▲ *Tyrannosaurus* was the terror of its day, with jaws measuring over four feet long and teeth like knives.

After three years at the site Brown returned to the skeleton of this unknown beast, with a full team of workers. He excavated it, crated it, and sent it on the long journey to New York.

Naming the Giant

In 1905, Henry Fairfield Osborn, director of palaeontology at the American Museum of Natural History, examined these bones. He realized what he was looking at. They were from a fearsome flesh-eating animal, far bigger than anything yet discovered. Osborn gave the animal an awesome genus (related group) name, *Tyrannosaurus*, meaning "tyrant reptile," and a species name, *rex*, meaning "king." Osborn and Brown had discovered *Tyrannosaurus rex*.

Find out more about the *Tyrannosaurus rex* story on pages 23–24.

◄ This full-size model shows *Tyrannosaurus rex* in a ferocious pose. At forty feet long, *Tyrannosaurus* towered over all other meat-eating dinosaurs.

The Story of *Iguanodon*

Tyrannosaurus rex was by no means the first dinosaur to be discovered. There were many important finds during the nineteenth century, one of which was made by an English country doctor—and avid fossil hunter—Gideon Mantell.

Around 1820, local quarry workers brought Dr. Mantell and his wife Mary Ann pieces of fossil bones and teeth that they had found in the local rocks, in Sussex, England. These rocks were formed about 130 million years ago during the early Cretaceous period. Mantell was convinced that these were pieces of a very large reptile. The problem was that this type of teeth belonged to a creature that ate plants. The famous scientists of the time, to whom Mantell showed the fossils, could not imagine such a big plant-eating reptile. They said that they were the remains of a mammal, such as a rhinoceros, or even some kind of fish.

Then, on a visit to the Hunterian Museum in London, Mantell met Samuel Stutchbury, who was studying iguanas—large, plant-eating lizards (a type of reptile) from South and Central America. Mantell noticed that his fossil teeth seemed to be giant versions of the teeth of this lizard. Perhaps he had found a reptile's teeth after all.

These two-inch long teeth alerted Mantell to a new kind of dinosaur—*Iguanodon*. ▼

Mantell's *Iguanodon*

From the bones and teeth that he had already found, Mantell made drawings of a big, lizard-like, plant-eating animal that could have been anywhere from fifty to two hundred feet long. He published his results in 1825 and called his animal *Iguanodon*, meaning "iguana-toothed."

Mantell always thought of the animal as being a big, four-footed beast. Scientists, and the public, soon accepted this big plant-eating lizard idea. Mantell collected many more *Iguanodon* remains during the rest of his life—so many, in fact, that his wife Mary Ann could stand no more and finally left him.

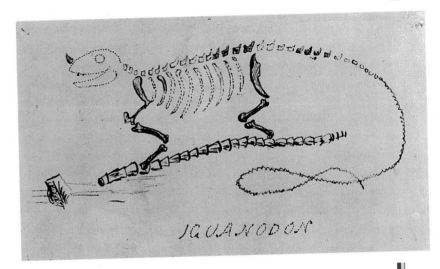

IGUANODON

▲ Mantell's sketch of an *Iguanodon*. Although he incorrectly placed the spikelike thumb bone on the nose, like a horn, the four-footed pose was proved to be correct in the 1980s.

The Belgian Connection

The next insight into the life of *Iguanodon* came in 1878. In February of that year coal miners working in the mines of Bernissart, in Belgium, broke through the coal face and found some very strange rocks. The mine director identified them as fossil bones. A local zoologist, P. J. Van Beneden, recognized *Iguanodon* teeth among them. The mine was closed while experts from the Royal Museum of Natural History in Brussels removed the fossils. What came out of that mine were 140 tons of rock containing no less than eleven complete and twenty almost complete *Iguanodon* skeletons.

Posing a Problem

An abandoned chapel near Brussels soon became a workshop. Louis Dollo, a palaeontologist from the Royal Museum, was called in to direct the studies and reconstructions of the bones into skeletons. He spent almost thirty years on the work. The bones were full of a mineral that reacted with air and destroyed the fossil; this meant preserving the bones was the first task. They were all sealed in a tarlike mixture of glue and plaster, which preserved them but covered up much of the fine detail. When the skeletons were put together, the hind (back) limbs appeared much longer than the front limbs. This suggested that the animal stood on its hind legs rather than on all fours, and so this was how the skeletons were mounted.

All this work gave us the image of *Iguanodon* that is still most familiar—a 33-foot-long animal, walking on its hind legs, heavy tail dragging on the ground, and feeding from high branches reached by a long neck.

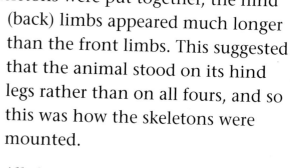

◄ **King Leopold of Belgium came to inspect the work and thought that the animals looked like some kind of giraffe. It was not a bad guess—they had long necks and long narrow heads, which were perfect for grazing in high trees.**

In the 1930s, the scientists in charge of the Belgian display noticed that the bones were still rotting, even under the original tarlike preservative. They then treated the bones with shellac, a kind of natural varnish, which worked better but still hid many of the details.

New Pose—Mantell Proved Right

Much later, in 1980, a British palaeontologist named David Norman looked at these skeletons again. Peering beneath the preservative, he found all sorts of things, such as a very complicated chewing mechanism that showed that *Iguanodon* had cheeks and a mouth like a cow—not a long slit of a mouth like a lizard. He also noticed that the tail looked all twisted and wrong when down on the ground, and that the "hand" had weight-bearing hooves on its "fingers." His conclusion was that, although it could rear up to reach leaves on high branches, *Iguanodon* was basically a four-footed animal. Mantell had been right all along.

The modern idea of *Iguanodon* is of a heavy animal that walked on all fours as an adult, but on two feet when a youngster. ▶

The Story of *Megalosaurus*

Megalosaurus, the big meat-eating dinosaur of Jurassic times (208–146 million years ago), lays claim to being the first dinosaur discovered and described, even though this was happening at about the same time that Mantell was picking up pieces of *Iguanodon*.

In 1822, William Buckland, a teacher of geology at Oxford University in England, was presented with a number of fossil bones. These included a piece of a jaw with sharp, bladelike teeth. The bones came from local quarries containing rocks dating from the Jurassic period. Because Buckland was busy at the time, he passed the remains over to a colleague, a medical man named James Parkinson. Parkinson came up with the name *Megalosaurus*, meaning "big lizard" or "big reptile," but did not study the remains in any detail.

A jawbone of *Megalosaurus*, with its meat-shearing teeth, similar to that studied by William Buckland. ▼

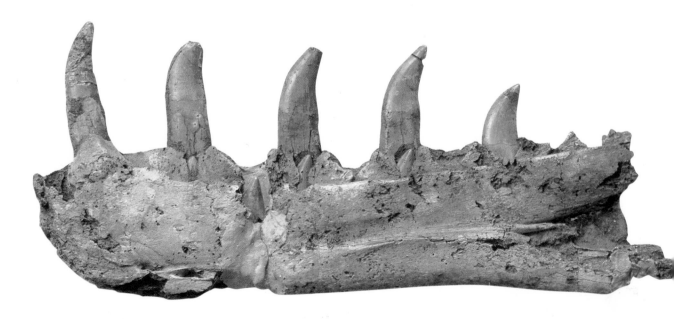

Dinosaur Excitement

William Buckland published the first detailed description of this *Megalosaurus* in 1824—a year before Mantell finally published his studies on *Iguanodon*. Mantell's *Iguanodon* and Buckland's *Megalosaurus* seemed to have a great deal in common. In 1832, Mantell found fragments of a big armored reptile, which he named *Hylaeosaurus*. This, too, seemed to belong to the same group of animals. These great reptiles were discussed with excitement at the annual meeting of the British Association for the Advancement of Science in 1841. Sir Richard Owen, a professor at the Royal College of Surgeons and an expert on animal anatomy, realized that they were very different from any other reptiles. In 1842, he suggested that they be placed in an animal category, or classification, of their own and proposed the name *Dinosauria* or "terrible lizards/reptiles" to describe them. Today we use the popular word *dinosaur*.

The Great Exhibition was opened in London in 1851 as a showcase of British technological achievement. Imagine the thrill for Victorian families—at the park at Crystal Palace, they were able to see the statues of these amazing, newly discovered creatures. ▼

The First Dinosaur Theme Park

The Great Exhibition of 1851 was a sort of world's fair in London. When it closed, the Crystal Palace—its centerpiece—was dismantled and rebuilt on a permanent site in Sydenham, south London. The surrounding park was planned as an entertainment and educational complex. Full-scale statues of the newly discovered dinosaurs were built on an island in one of the lakes in the park.

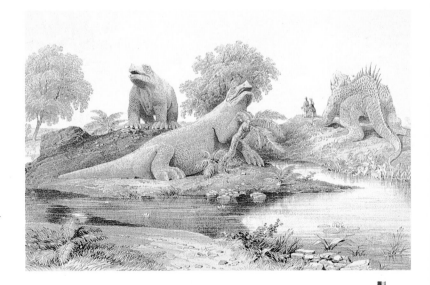

The first dinosaur theme park was born. Sir Richard Owen oversaw the project. The models were created by the sculptor Benjamin Waterhouse Hawkins. As well as the dinosaurs, there were models of prehistoric sea reptiles, such as plesiosaurs and ichthyosaurs, and also some of the strange mammals that came later. In all, models of 33 extinct animals were built, and the exhibition was opened by Queen Victoria in 1854.

Megalosaurus **was typical of the meat-eating dinosaurs. It walked on its hind limbs, its big head held forward and balanced by the heavy tail. ▼**

Megalosaurus Muddle

Although *Megalosaurus* was the first recognized dinosaur, not a great deal is known about it even now.

In the early days of palaeontology, any bone fragment that looked as if it had come from a meat-eating dinosaur was called *Megalosaurus*. Over the years this has caused confusion in identifying *Megalosaurus*.

The most complete skeleton thought to be of a *Megalosaurus* was found near Oxford in 1926. The skeleton was first studied by the German palaeontologist Friedrich von Huene, who declared it to be a *Megalosaurus*.

It was not until 1964, when it was studied again by Alick Walker of Newcastle University, England, that scientists saw that the jaw was different from the original *Megalosaurus* jaws and teeth, which Buckland had described. This almost complete skeleton is now called *Eustreptospondylus*, and all that we know of the true *Megalosaurus* is a handful of bones and teeth.

The Story of *Hadrosaurus*

The great dinosaur discoveries of the second half of the nineteenth century were mostly in the United States and Canada.

In the 1850s, some big bones were uncovered by quarry workers digging in cretaceous rock near the town of Haddonfield, New Jersey. Nobody paid them much attention until William Foulke, a member of the Academy of Natural Sciences in Philadelphia, heard about them while he was on vacation nearby. He gained permission to dig in the quarry himself and found a mass of enormous bones. He sent these to the Academy, where Dr. Joseph Leidy identified them as dinosaur bones in 1858. Leidy named this dinosaur *Hadrosaurus*, meaning "sturdy lizard."

This was a much more complete skeleton than any that had been found before. Leidy saw right away that the hind legs were much longer than the front legs. He was the first to realize that most dinosaurs usually walked on their hind legs.

The group of dinosaurs called hadrosaurs are often referred to as the "duck-billed dinosaurs." This hadrosaur skull shows a ducklike beak. ▼

Parasaurolophus
▼

Hadrosaurus

Lambeosaurus

Kritosaurus

▲ **Hadrosaurs were placid (peaceful) plant-eaters.**

The Unfinished Theme Park

Benjamin Waterhouse Hawkins, the sculptor who created the Crystal Palace statues, accepted an invitation from New York City to create a similar scene in Central Park, but with North American dinosaurs. Hawkins went to work, touring the museums and studying North American fossils. The only other North American dinosaur known at that time was a beast called *Laelaps*, a big-clawed meat-eater, which was discovered in 1866. The centerpiece of Hawkins's display was to have been a fight between the plant-eating *Hadrosaurus* and a pack of hunting *Laelaps*.

Unfortunately, in 1871, the City of New York was in financial trouble. The people in charge of the parks decided not to go ahead with the statue park. After three years of work, a horrified Hawkins saw his statues, molds, and equipment smashed to pieces and buried deep in a corner of Central Park.

The Bone Wars— Cope and Marsh

Two men dominate the story of dinosaur discoveries toward the end of the nineteenth century. They were Americans and their names were Edward Drinker Cope and Othniel Charles Marsh. They both led expeditions into the wilderness of North America hunting dinosaur remains. While their missions were similar, and their goals were the same, the two men became great rivals.

Cope had studied anatomy with Joseph Leidy in Philadelphia, but apart from that he was a self-taught palaeontologist. Although very intelligent, he had little patience and was often rude to other people.

Marsh studied at Yale University. He raised a great deal of money for the university and was made professor there. However, he became very protective of his finds and did not want to share the credit for discoveries.

From Friendship to Rivalry

The two men had started as friends, but this friendship did not last. In 1869, Cope wrote a scientific paper on a plesiosaur—a long-necked, short-tailed swimming reptile. Unfortunately, he put the head on the wrong end, making it a short-necked, long-tailed swimming reptile. Gleefully, Marsh pointed out the mistake. This created bad feelings between the two men that never went away.

Prospecting for Bones

In the 1870s, as the west of America was being settled by people from the East Coast and Europe, many pioneers began to notice the huge bones that lay in the ground in particular areas. Arthur Lakes, a schoolteacher in Colorado, wrote to Othniel Marsh, telling him of the fossil bones he had found near the town of Morrison. Lakes then sent him a shipment of the bones themselves. When Marsh was slow to reply, Lakes sent another shipment, but this time to Edward Cope.

As soon as Marsh heard that Cope had been contacted, he sent his chief field collector, a large man named Ben Mudge, to make sure that Lakes dealt only with him. At the same time O. W. Lucas, another teacher, wrote to Cope about a discovery of bones at Canon City, also in Colorado. Cope commissioned Lucas to dig for more, and so Lucas opened a quarry. When Marsh's man Mudge saw that Lucas was finding better dinosaurs for Cope than Mudge was finding for Marsh, Mudge set up a rival quarry at Canon City. This was in 1877. The "bone wars" had begun.

Marsh, (center, back row), led many expeditions into the West. The hammer Marsh holds is for digging out fossils. But the others in the group carry rifles, handguns, and knives—to deal with any "problems" that come up while on the hunt for fossils. ▶

▲ A painting by Arthur Lakes showing work at Como Bluff

Now it was known that both scientists wanted to find dinosaur fossils, and both were willing to pay for them. Two railroadmen, William Reed and William Carlin, wrote to Marsh about bones they had found while working on the Union Pacific Railroad, which was being built westward toward the Rocky Mountains. They mentioned that if Marsh was not interested, somebody else would be, meaning Edward Cope. Marsh immediately sent them a check, but it did them no good. They had used false names because they had been looking for bones during work time, and so they could not cash it!

The find by Reed and Carlin, at a hill in Wyoming called Como Bluff, turned out to be one of the greatest dinosaur sites in North America. All these sites—Como Bluff, Canon City, and the Morrison town area—were sites of late Jurassic rocks formed on river flood plains where dinosaurs had roamed. The sequence of Jurassic rock, which stretches from New Mexico to Montana, was to be known as the Morrison Formation after the first site.

◄ This map of the U.S. shows the area of the Morrison Formation (in green).

Outright War

The incidents during the bone wars became more and more dramatic. Cope disguised himself and spied on his rival's excavation at Como Bluff. Marsh's workers, Carlin and Reed, argued, and Carlin ran off and joined Cope's workers. Marsh's party, after excavating all they could from a site, began smashing up everything left so it would not fall into Cope's hands. On one occasion, Reed positioned himself above Cope's excavations and sent landslides down to fill in the site as quickly as the workers were excavating it.

Good Finds from Bad Feelings

The positive outcome of Cope's and Marsh's fierce rivalry was their incredible accomplishment: the two of them uncovered over 130 new types of dinosaur.

Othniel Marsh is credited with the discovery of _Triceratops_, although Edward Cope discovered parts of it too. This led to further disagreement between them. ▼

As the two men grew older, the bitterness continued. They both died, enemies to the end, before the turn of the century. The behavior of Marsh and Cope may have set a bad example for palaeontologists, but their discoveries greatly increased our knowledge of dinosaurs in a short space of time.

The Story of *Archaeopteryx*

In 1859, Charles Darwin (1809–82) had published his theories on evolution. It sparked tremendous debate. According to most religions, a divine creator had made animal and human life in a short time. Darwin's theory stated that life evolved over millions of years.

"Soft" Fossils and the Evolution Question

In 1861, in a limestone quarry in Germany, workers found a fossil feather. This is unusual, since soft materials, such as feathers, are rarely fossilized. But this was a very fine limestone, and all sorts of soft things such as worms, jellyfish, and the wings of flying reptiles were being found as fossils.

A month or so after the first find, an almost complete fossil of a feathered creature was found. As described by Germany's foremost palaeontologist, Hermann von Meyer, this animal combined the long tail and clawed hands of a reptile with the feathers and wishbone (collarbone) of a bird. If birds had evolved from reptiles, this was obviously the in-between form between the two. He called this animal *Archaeopteryx*—meaning "ancient wing." This specimen ended up in the Natural History Museum in London. It is now known as the London specimen.

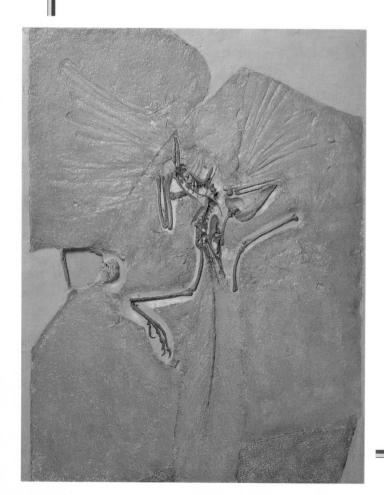

The London specimen of *Archaeopteryx*, which shows hands and feathered tail—see the picture on page 22. ▼

After the feather and the London specimen, a third specimen turned up in the same quarries in 1877 and eventually came to be known as the Berlin specimen. This was even more complete, with the skull and jaws in place. It was the skull of a bird, but it had reptile-like teeth in the jaws. No others were found until 1956. To date a total of eight *Archaeopteryx* specimens exist—including the first feather—all found in the same region and in varying degrees of completeness.

Creationists are people who believe in the Bible's account of the creation of all things. One of the supporters of Darwin's theory of evolution was the British scientist, Thomas Henry Huxley. In the 1860s, when defending *Archaeopteryx* against the arguments of the Creationists, Huxley stated that *Archaeopteryx* showed that birds evolved from dinosaurs.

The Berlin specimen of *Archaeopteryx* with complete skull and wings. It is on display at the Humboldt University Museum in Berlin, Germany. ▶

This idea was rejected by Danish palaeontologist Gerhard Heilmann in the 1920s, who preferred to think that *Archaeopteryx* had had the same reptile ancestor as the dinosaurs, but the two had developed along different lines. This was the accepted view until 1973, when American palaeontologist John Ostrom raised the question again. He found bird-like features in the hips and legs of many small meat-eating dinosaurs and many dinosaur features in the reptilian parts of *Archaeopteryx*. As if to confirm this, the seventh *Archaeopteryx* specimen was identified in 1987. It had lain in someone's collection for twenty years, labeled as a small dinosaur, until the feathers were finally noticed.

Now most scientists accept that *Archaeopteryx*, and hence the whole bird line, evolved from dinosaurs. Some even go so far as to regard modern birds as feathered dinosaurs. Perhaps the dinosaurs did not die out—they just changed!

◄ **Without the hands and teeth, *Archaeopteryx* would have looked like a modern bird. Here is a drawing of how the creature might have looked in life.**

The Continuing Story of *Tyrannosaurus Rex*

Barnum Brown and Henry Fairfield Osborn were very pleased with themselves when they found and described *Tyrannosaurus rex* in 1905 (see pages 4–5). They continued working, hoping to uncover better and more complete specimens. This they did in 1907. The new one was largely complete, except for the limbs and parts of the tail, and it took Brown's team three summers to excavate it. The jaws alone were encased in a stone block that weighed over five tons. This is the skeleton that is now mounted in the American Museum of Natural History in New York. The way it was originally mounted was wrong. The scientists had to use guesswork—the tail was too long, the front limbs had three instead of two fingers, and the back sloped at an angle of 45 degrees.

Barnum Brown (right) and Henry Fairfield Osborn digging up a section of the tail of a *Diplodocus* in 1897. They worked together many times, and are most famous for their *Tyrannosaurus rex* discoveries. ▶

Who Owns "Sue"?

So far only 16 specimens of *Tyrannosaurus* have been found, and most of those have turned up since 1980. One of the biggest and most complete was found in 1990 by Susan Hendrickson in South Dakota while out hiking. She alerted her colleagues Peter and Neal Larson from the Black Hills Institute, a fossil research organization. They got permission from the landowner and excavated the entire skeleton, now called "Sue" after its discoverer.

Then trouble struck! The Sioux Nation (a Native American tribe) claimed that it owned the land on which it was found. So the Sioux sued for "Sue." But then the U.S. government decided that the skeleton was government property, and that none of them—the Black Hills Institute, the original landowner, or the Sioux—had any right to it. On May 14, 1992 the FBI, the National Guard, and U.S. Marshals, armed like one of Cope's or Marsh's field parties, mounted a dawn raid on the Institute and confiscated the whole skeleton—still encased in 11 tons of rock.

The issue still has not been cleared up. The Larsons of the Black Hills Institute could face a long prison sentence and fines of over $13 million. For now, the biggest and best *Tyrannosaurus* skeleton lies locked in a basement storeroom under armed guard.

▲ It takes skill to extract, clean, and put together a dinosaur skeleton. This palaeontologist is working on a *Tyrannosaurus*'s tail.

Canada—A Land of Dinosaur Opportunity

By the beginning of this century Barnum Brown's success was at its peak. His exploration of the Cretaceous rocks of the northern United States took him farther north into Canada. There he opened an extremely rich area of dinosaur deposits along the Red Deer River, in Alberta. He managed to do this by equipping a barge as an excavation base and sailing it along the river, exploring the sides of the gorge as he went. The remains of dinosaurs such as *Centrosaurus* and *Corythosaurus* began to see the light of day after 70 million years.

A magnificent *Tyrannosaurus rex* skeleton. It is on display at the Tyrrell Museum of Palaeontology, in Alberta, Canada. The museum is named after Joseph Burr Tyrrell, the Canadian geologist who had first noticed dinosaur remains in the area in the 1880s. ▼

The Search in Alberta

Brown's success spurred the Canadian authorities to mount their own expeditions. In 1912, fossil hunter Charles Sternberg was dispatched by the Geological Survey of Canada to the same area to find dinosaurs for Canadian museums. Sternberg had learned his craft from Edward Cope during the "bone wars."

The area proved to be so rich in fossils that it eventually yielded about ten percent of all the dinosaur types known to date and is still being explored today. The area is now protected as a World Heritage Site.

The Great Sauropods

Sauropod is the name given to the group of long-necked, plant-eating dinosaurs, such as *Diplodocus* and *Apatosaurus*.

Map showing the area where Earl Douglass worked in Utah. It is now called the Dinosaur National Monument. ▼

In 1902, Earl Douglass, a palaeontologist from the Carnegie Museum in Pittsburgh, Pennsylvania, went to the Morrison Formation area in Utah in search of dinosaur remains. Eventually, he came across the tail bones of something huge sticking out of a cliff. After some digging he realized that there was an almost-complete skeleton there. Knowing it would take some time to excavate such a thing, he built a permanent camp and moved his wife and children in so that he could be at the site summer and winter. What Douglass excavated first was an *Apatosaurus*.

This was not the first *Apatosaurus* to be found, but it was the first good one. The first had been found and named by Othniel Marsh in 1877. In 1904, Douglass found another, more complete skeleton, which he named *Brontosaurus*, not realizing that the two animals were the same. This *Brontosaurus*, its powerful name meaning "thunder lizard," caught the public's imagination. It was not until well into the twentieth century that it was realized that the two skeletons were of the same beast. The rules about scientific names are strict, and when two names have been given to the same animal, the first name given is accepted as correct. So the dramatic *Brontosaurus* had to give way to the much more ordinary *Apatosaurus*—meaning "mysterious lizard."

Douglass and Marsh—A Clash of Heads

Apatosaurus is a typical sauropod. The head was tiny and, as with most dinosaurs, the skull was very fragile and rarely fossilized. This led to another confusion over *Apatosaurus* (or *Brontosaurus*).

Neither of Marsh's skeletons had skulls. He assumed that the skull would be like that of *Camarasaurus*, another sauropod that lived at the same time. As a result, any *Apatosaurus* skeleton mounted in a museum carried a plaster skull like that of *Camarasaurus*.

Douglass knew better. Among the many remains that he found in Utah was the skull of *Apatosaurus*. It was not squat and boxy, like that of *Camarasaurus*, but long and narrow, like that of *Diplodocus*, another local sauropod. However, Earl Douglass was not well known enough to challenge the great Othniel Charles Marsh. No one listened to Douglass. It was not until 1979 that the mistake was noted, and Douglass was shown to be right. The skull of *Apatosaurus* in the Carnegie Museum was finally replaced with a more appropriate one.

The long necks of sauropods, such as *Camarasaurus*, *Diplodocus*, and *Apatosaurus*, were ideal for reaching the leaves of tall trees. ▼

Apatosaurus

Diplodocus

Camarasaurus

▲ Today, at the Dinosaur National Monument, work continues in Douglass's original quarry.

Douglass's Legacy

Douglass lived on the Utah site, sending back dinosaur skeletons until 1923, when the Carnegie Museum decided that it had enough and canceled the order. Douglass, however, stayed on and continued digging for other museums. The site is now the Dinosaur National Monument, and the public can watch scientists studying the fossils embedded in the rock.

Changing Ideas

For most of the century it was believed that *Apatosaurus*, *Diplodocus*, *Camarasaurus,* and the other sauropods were too heavy to live on land. They were always illustrated partially submerged in swamps, where the water could buoy up their weight. Footprint evidence (see pages 40–41) was always against this, but not until the 1970s was it accepted that sauropods lived on land, moving about in herds like elephants.

Ideas about the behavior of dinosaurs are changing all the time, and so are ideas about their appearance. It was always thought that sauropods dragged their tails along the ground. Then, in the 1970s, British zoologist R. McNeill Alexander looked at the way the backbone was supported. He came to the conclusion that the tail was held high in the air.

In 1992, American palaeontologist Stephen Czerkas found evidence that sauropod skin was scaly and not leathery and wrinkled like an elephant's, as had been believed. We have known about sauropods for 120 years, and we are still finding out new things about them.

The Tendaguru Expedition

The story of the hunt for dinosaurs, and particularly for big sauropods, now moves to Africa.

The country known as Tanzania was called German East Africa at the beginning of this century. Eberhard Fraas, a German palaeontologist, took an account of fossil bones, found in a remote area called Tendaguru, back to Germany with him. In 1909, the Berlin Museum set about organizing an expedition to excavate in the area under the leadership of Werner Janensch.

The excavation took four years and involved the hiring of several hundred local people as laborers. Each discovery had to be carried down to the coast by porters. During this time about 275 tons of material was shipped back to Berlin.

The prize of this expedition was the skeleton of a sauropod, *Brachiosaurus*. It was the biggest skeleton found at the time. *Brachiosaurus* was over 75 feet long, with a head that towered 40 feet above the ground. A skeleton of *Brachiosaurus* had already been found in Morrison Formation rocks in North America, but not such a complete one.

From the port of Dar es Salaam it took two days by steamboat to the closest landing point on the African coast, followed by four days' trek to Tendaguru itself. All the equipment was carried by porters. ▼

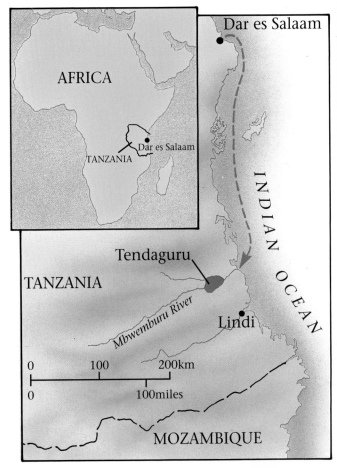

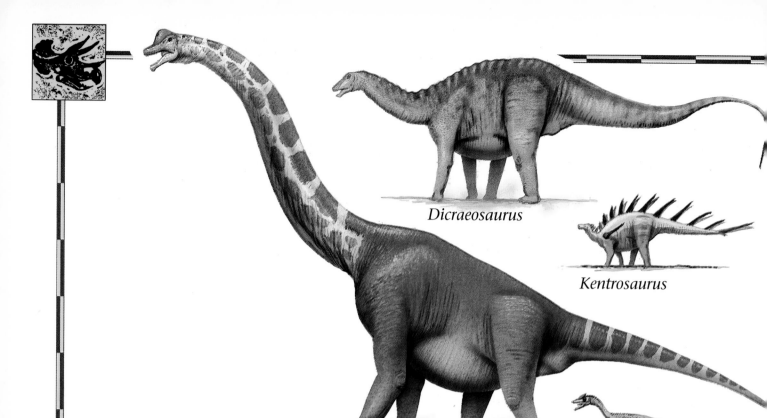

Dicraeosaurus

Kentrosaurus

Dryosaurus   *Brachiosaurus*   *Elaphrosaurus*

▲ The expedition in east Africa found dinosaurs that were similiar to those found in North America, such as: *Dicraeosaurus*, a sauropod closely related to *Diplodocus*; *Kentrosaurus*, related to *Stegosaurus*; *Dryosaurus*, a small plant eater similar to those found at the Morrison Formation; and *Elaphrosaurus*, a fast-moving meat eater.

Dinosaur Discoveries—Proof of Continental Drift?

The similarity between this collection of African fossils and the North American fossils indicates that the same conditions existed in North America and East Africa in late Jurassic times, and also that the two areas were once on the same landmass. In 1909, the idea of continental drift had not become accepted, so this was new proof.

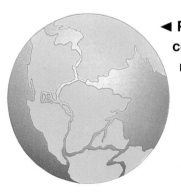

◄ Position of continents 200 million years ago

Present position of continents ►

The Gobi Desert Expeditions

The biggest scientific land expedition to leave the United States was led by Roy Chapman Andrews of the American Museum of Natural History. His team set off into the wilderness of the Gobi Desert, in Mongolia, part of China, in the early months of 1922.

Forty scientists and helpers, with their supplies carried on trucks and camels, set off into the desert with no clear idea of where they were going or what they were searching for. There was an idea going around a few years previously that the origins of *Homo sapiens* (modern humans) would be found in Central Asia. The massive expedition set out with the vague instruction to find proof of this.

Andrews and his assistant George Olsen with their amazing nest of dinosaur eggs. ▼

What the expedition did find, however, was one of the most exciting dinosaur discoveries ever. The scientists brought back fossil material from several places along the route. After the material had been studied in the American Museum of Natural History by Henry Fairfield Osborn, the scientists were told go back next season and get some more.

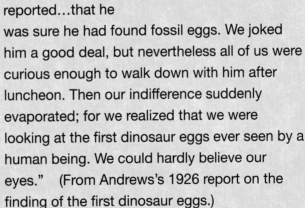

"Our real thrill came on the second day, when George Olsen reported…that he was sure he had found fossil eggs. We joked him a good deal, but nevertheless all of us were curious enough to walk down with him after luncheon. Then our indifference suddenly evaporated; for we realized that we were looking at the first dinosaur eggs ever seen by a human being. We could hardly believe our eyes."   (From Andrews's 1926 report on the finding of the first dinosaur eggs.)

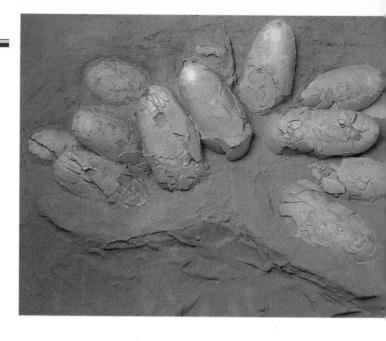

Excitement about Eggs

There were five expeditions during the 1920s, and the best material was found at a spectacular rock face the scientists named Flaming Cliffs. A primitive horned dinosaur, *Protoceratops*, was found there, but the most exciting thing was the discovery of dinosaur nests, complete with eggs. Until then it had only been guessed that dinosaurs laid eggs. Here, at last, was the actual proof.

Other finds also shed light on the lifestyles of the dinosaurs. A small meat-eating *Oviraptor* was discovered close to the nests. It was a strange little animal, with jaws that seemed to be adapted for breaking into eggs. Also found was the vicious hunter *Velociraptor*, with its curved hind claw, which was used as a killing tool. It was clear that the dinosaur nests were a target for egg thieves and the *Protoceratops* were prey for hunting beasts. This last point was proved when an expedition to the site, in 1971, found skeletons of a *Velociraptor* and a *Protoceratops* locked in a struggle that had killed them both.

▲ The eggs found by Roy Chapman Andrews. They were laid 88 million years ago, during the Cretaceous period. Originally they were thought to be *Protoceratops* eggs, but a later examination showed that they were actually *Oviraptor* eggs.

Whose Eggs?

It had always been thought that the nests belonged to *Protoceratops*. But in 1994 one of the eggs was opened and inside was—not a *Protoceratops* but a baby *Oviraptor*! The *Oviraptor* found with the original nest had not been stealing eggs—it had been in its own nest all the time.

The Dinosaur Debate—Warm- or Cold-Blooded?

Not all exciting discoveries are made in the remote wilderness by travel-worn field-workers. Much important work is done by researchers in the laboratory, such as Robert T. Bakker, at Harvard University.

In the early 1970s, when Bakker was a research student, he studied the numbers of plant-eating dinosaurs that had been found and the numbers of meat eaters in the same area. He came up with a startling idea—dinosaurs were not sluggish cold-blooded animals like modern reptiles; they were active, warm-blooded creatures like modern mammals and birds.

The terms cold-blooded and warm-blooded are somewhat misleading. *Cold-blooded* means that the animal is at the same temperature as its surroundings, and is only active when the weather is warm enough. *Warm-blooded* means that the animal can stay at the same temperature, and remain active whatever the surrounding conditions. To do this, a warm-blooded animal needs to eat about ten times as much food as a cold-blooded animal. A warm-blooded, meat-eating dinosaur would need to eat a lot more food than a cold-blooded meat eater. After studying the number of meat eaters, Bakker concluded that dinosaurs, the meat eaters at least, were warm-blooded.

Bakker's other evidence included the dinosaurs' vast rib cages—big enough to contain huge hearts and lungs—and blood vessels in the bones that would give a swift supply of blood for an active lifestyle.

Bakker's ideas were backed up by John Ostrom, who had in 1964 discovered the skeleton of *Deinonychus* in Montana. The more he studied the skeleton of this vicious tiger-sized meat eater, the more he found similarities to the skeletons of birds. It balanced on long hind legs and held its body parallel to the ground, like an ostrich. The killing claw on the hind foot was as mobile as that of an eagle. When it fought it would have done so with its feet, like a fighting rooster. All this suggested that *Deinonychus* was warm-blooded, like a bird.

The idea of active, warm-blooded dinosaurs caught the public's imagination. Now dinosaurs were beginning to change appearance. Scientists and artists began to give them furry or feathery coats, something for which there was no evidence, but was suggested by a warm-blooded lifestyle.

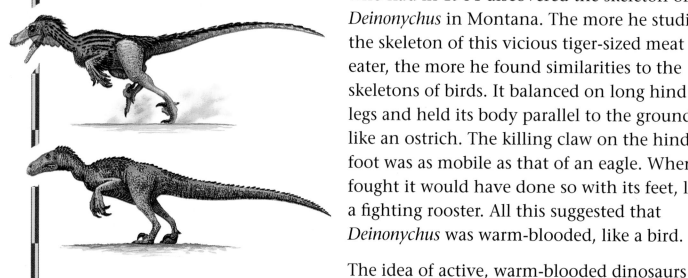

▲ Top: *Deinonychus* with feathers, as an active, warm-blooded creature as described by John Ostrom. Below: How *Deinonychus* may have looked if it had been a cold-blooded dinosaur.

The Debate Continues

Other scientists disagreed with this theory, finding as much evidence against warm-bloodedness as Bakker was finding for it. Some scientists proposed a compromise—dinosaurs were neither fully warm-blooded nor cold-blooded but somewhere between the two. That is how the matter stands at the moment.

The Story of *Stegosaurus*

Even when a dinosaur skeleton is almost complete there is plenty of room for interpretation and guesswork.

Confusion over Plates

Stegosaurus, for instance, is known from two complete and several not-so-complete skeletons. Othniel Charles Marsh first drew a *Stegosaurus* skeleton in 1891. Because the drawing showed the side of the dinosaur, it seemed to have one row of plates of bone down its back. The first artists to paint a *Stegosaurus* therefore gave it a single row of plates, despite the fact that Marsh's written descriptions clearly mentioned a double row.

Marsh's *Stegosaurus* seemed to show only a single row of plates along its back. ▼

Edward Drinker Cope also published research on *Stegosaurus* and mentioned two rows of plates—the only thing that the two ever agreed upon. However, there was still confusion about whether the plates were arranged in neat pairs or staggered on the left and right sides. Even the best fossils do not help. When found, *Stegosaurus* skeletons were lying on their sides, and their plates had come loose and fallen at odd angles.

The Purpose of the Plates

It was originally thought that the plates were armor of some sort. In that case, they would have been most useful lying flat on the animal's back. But with the idea of warm-blooded dinosaurs in the 1970s came the suggestion that the plates were covered in skin and acted as heat exchangers, warming the blood when turned to the sun or cooling it when held into the wind. That would make more sense with alternating vertical plates. The plates are full of blood vessels, suggesting that this theory could be true. But if the plates were armor and covered with horn they would be full of blood vessels, too. To add to the confusion, other stegosaurs, such as the African *Kentrosaurus* and the British *Lexovisaurus*, had spines, not plates, arranged in pairs.

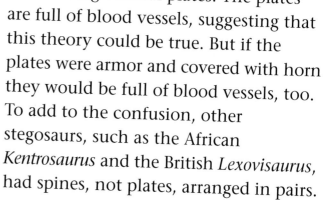

The last clue is from a *Stegosaurus* found in 1992 by Brian Small from the University of California, Berkeley. It shows that the plates were arranged in a double alternating row, but the spikes on the end of the tail pointed outward. So this is the accepted view—until the next find...

◄ A mounted *Stegosaurus* skeleton showing the two rows of bone plates. *Stegosaurus* could stand on its hind legs. That is another recent discovery. The strength of the backbone in the hip region would have enabled it to do this.

The Family Story—Nesting and Herding Dinosaurs

If dinosaurs were reptiles, then they would have laid eggs in the sand and gone off and left them, just like many modern reptiles do. That was what everybody assumed after Roy Chapman Andrews found the dinosaur nests in the Gobi Desert in the 1920s.

The second set of dinosaur eggs to be found seemed to support this. In 1930, dinosaur eggs were seen in the rock of a hillside in Aix-en-Provence, in southern France, along with bones of the sauropod *Hypselosaurus*. The eggs were grapefruit-shaped, 12 inches in diameter, and laid in pairs, possibly as the animal had walked along.

A Chance Discovery

In 1978, two palaeontologists, John Horner and Bob Makela, were in Montana, hunting for dinosaur fossils. They stopped at a fossil shop to see what the collectors had been gathering, and the shopkeeper brought out a tray of tiny fossil bone fragments. Horner suspected that these were bones of baby hadrosaurs, later called *Maiasaura*. Tracing back to the hillside where these were found, Horner and Makela uncovered a nest full of dinosaur chicks.

John Horner with the shell and skeleton cast of a baby *Maiasaura*. The nest is full of the eggs of *Orodromeus*, a dinosaur like a small *Iguanodon*. ▶

37

The remarkable thing was that the chicks were not newly hatched—they were partly grown.

This meant that they had remained in the nest for some time after they had hatched. It also meant that one or both parent dinosaurs must have looked after them like parent birds do. This suggested that dinosaurs had family lives!

▲ A newly hatched *Maiasaura* baby would have been rather helpless, as the size of the skeleton suggests. The parent dinosaur would have had to take care of it.

▲ The skeleton of a young *Maiasaura*

Good Mother

For the next few years John Horner and Bob Makela and their team excavated the site, now called Egg Mountain. They found other nests and skeletons of various sizes. It was clear that these dinosaurs nested in herds, coming back to the same site every year. The animal concerned was a 33-foot hadrosaur that they called *Maiasaura* meaning "good mother lizard."

Nobody had found this kind of evidence for family behavior before because they had been looking in the wrong places. They were looking for dinosaur fossils in rocks that had been laid down in river flood plains and in swamps—good places for dinosaurs to live. The nests were found in rocks that had been formed by lakes in upland regions. Dinosaurs probably migrated in herds between the two regions in different seasons.

Scientists were beginning to realize that dinosaurs behaved more like mammals than reptiles.

In late Cretaceous times North America was alive with family groups and herds of dinosaurs, such as these hadrosaurs. ▼

What Footprints Tell Us

Brownstone buildings—the sandstone housing of nineteenth century New York City—were mostly built from sandstones quarried from nearby Connecticut. For years the quarry workers had found strange, three-toed footprints in these rocks dating from the Triassic period (245–208 million years ago). They looked very much like the footprints of birds.

Edward Hitchcock, an American geologist, was the first person to do any sort of scientific study on these. In 1835, he announced that these prints had been made by a kind of gigantic bird that had once existed in the area. This was six years before the term "dinosaurs" had been coined.

It was Thomas Huxley who noted the birdlike form of the feet of the first dinosaurs to be discovered and concluded that these tracks in Connecticut had actually been made by dinosaurs.

Following the Footsteps

Some of the most famous footprints were found in Texas in the 1940s, by Roland T. Bird of the American Museum of Natural History. He followed the directions given to him from staff at a Native American trading post where fossils were sold, and discovered tracks of a big sauropod, such as *Apatosaurus*, being followed by a meat eater like *Allosaurus*. We say "such as" here because it is almost impossible to match a particular set of footprints to a particular dinosaur.

This is a photograph of the tracks found by Roland T. Bird in the 1940s. ▼

In 1960, an international team of scientists studying the geology of Spitsbergen, inside the Arctic Circle and only 600 miles from the North Pole, found a dinosaur trackway snaking up a cliff. In the next brief Arctic summer they went prepared with scaffolding and molding materials. The prints turned out to be from an *Iguanodon*-like dinosaur. It was the first clue that dinosaurs had lived so far north.

Dinosaur footprints usually cause less excitement than dinosaur skeletons. In the past, when footprints were discovered, they might have been reported and studied for a while, but then forgotten, left in the ground to be covered up by sand.

Clues in the Tracks

In fact, palaeontologists are now finding that dinosaur trackways are extremely important in helping to work out the lifestyles and habits of these ancient beasts. They can show if dinosaurs lived alone or in herds, how quickly they walked, whether they lived in swamps or dry land, or even if many different types lived together.

Now scientists are going back to try to rediscover trackways that were first found years ago and have since been lost.

These tracks in Arizona were lost after Roland T. Bird studied them in the 1940s. In the 1990s scientists had to use photographs of the landscape to find them again. ▼

The End of the Dinosaurs

In 1973, American scientist Walter Alvarez was deep in the limestone gorges of northern Italy studying the changes in rock layers. Alvarez came across something that was to have far-reaching effects. A band of clay lay in the otherwise regular limestone, and this clay was laid down as the Cretaceous period ended and the Cenozoic period began, 65 million years ago—just at the time that the dinosaurs had disappeared.

Alvarez and his father, Luis, a well-known scientist, studied this clay back at the laboratory and found it to be full of iridium—a material that is rare on the Earth's surface but very common in meteorites and comets in space. A check on rocks of the same period in other parts of the world showed that the layer of iridium-rich clay was seen worldwide.

▲ Walter Alvarez (right) and his father Luis, looking for evidence to show why the dinosaurs died out.

Theories on the End

Some scientists concluded that Earth was struck by a giant meteorite or a swarm of comets about 65 million years ago. This may have sent up so much smoke and debris that it blotted out the sun and changed the climate. This may have wiped out a large amount of plant and animal life—including the dinosaurs.

Other theories were given to account for the iridium, such as increased volcanic activity. So the existence of this material may have nothing to do with rocks from space at the time of the dinosaurs' extinction.

How and why dinosaurs became extinct is just one of the dinosaur mysteries that have still to be solved. Palaeontologists themselves tend not to be too concerned about dinosaur extinction. There is so much yet to be discovered about what the dinosaurs were like when they were alive—we probably only know of about a fifth of all the species that existed. Every year, every week, even every day, palaeontologists in the field and scientists in labs are adding more to our knowledge of the dinosaurs, the most exciting animals of all time.

Time Line

TRIASSIC PERIOD 245–208 million years ago	JURASSIC PERIOD 208–146 million years ago

239 m. years ago Early fernlike plants died out and were replaced by coniferous trees. Primitive reptiles that fed on them died out too, leaving room for the dinosaurs to evolve.

225 m. years ago First dinosaur.

156–146 m. years ago *Archaeopteryx*.

156–146 m. years ago Dinosaurs from the North American Morrison Formation—*Camarasaurus, Diplodocus, Apatosaurus, Stegosaurus, Allosaurus*.

JURASSIC PERIOD 208–146 million years ago	

175–155 m. years ago *Megalosaurus*.

169–156 m. years ago *Lexovisaurus*.

165 m. years ago *Eustreptospondylus*.

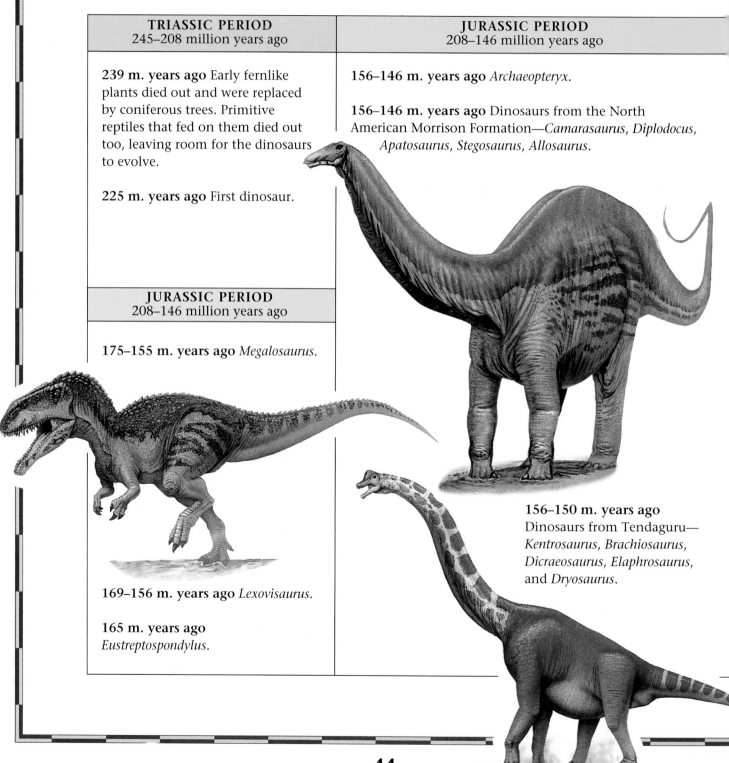

156–150 m. years ago Dinosaurs from Tendaguru—*Kentrosaurus, Brachiosaurus, Dicraeosaurus, Elaphrosaurus,* and *Dryosaurus*.

Dinosaurs have been known to us for less than two centuries, a minute period of time compared with the 160 million years that they existed.

CRETACEOUS PERIOD 146–65 million years ago	MODERN TIMES 1822–present
135–110 m. years ago Dinosaurs from the Weald of southern England—*Iguanodon*, *Hylaeosaurus*, *Hypsilophodon*. **119–93 m. years ago** *Deinonychus*. **88–77 m. years ago** Dinosaurs from the Gobi Desert—*Protoceratops*, *Oviraptor*, *Velociraptor*. **77–73 m. years ago** *Maiasaura* and *Orodromeus*. **76–73 m. years ago** *Hadrosaurus*. **75–72 m. years ago** *Lambeosaurus*. **76–65 m. years ago** *Parasaurolophus* and *Kritosarus*. **73–65 m. years ago** *Hypselosaurus*. **68–65 m. years ago** *Triceratops*. **68–65 m. years ago** *Tyrannosaurus*.	**1822** Parkinson named *Megalosaurus*. **1824** Buckland described *Megalosaurus*. **1825** Mantell described *Iguanodon*. **1842** Owen invented the name *Dinosauria*, or dinosaur. **1858** Leidy described *Hadrosaurus*. **1877–97** The "bone war" between Cope and Marsh. **1878** Over thirty *Iguanodon* skeletons found in Belgium. **1909–13** The German expeditions to Tendaguru, Africa. **1922–25** The American expeditions to the Gobi Desert, China. **1930s** China found to have rich and varied dinosaur remains. **1940s** R. T. Bird finds footprint fossils in Texas. **1970s** South America found to have rich and varied dinosaur remains. **1990s** First dinosaurs found in Antarctica.

Glossary

Adapted Changed or designed for a use.

Anatomy The study of how a living thing is put together.

Armored Covered with a hard protective outer layer.

Chewing mechanism How the jaw and facial muscles work together in order to chew food.

Comet A mass of ice and rock that drifts in space.

Continental drift The movement of continents across the surface of the earth. Two hundred million years ago the continents were one landmass but have drifted apart into their present positions.

Evolution The gradual change in the characteristics of a population of animals or plants over thousands or millions of years. Darwin's theory was that the species of animals and plants found in modern times were the result of ancient animals evolving.

Extinct The term used when a species of animal or plant has died out.

Fossil The remains of any living thing found preserved in the rocks.

Geology The study of the earth, such as rocks, fossils, and the history of the changing conditions at the earth's surface.

Mammal Warm-blooded animals that feed milk to their young.

Meteorite A lump of rock that falls to Earth from space.

Migrated To have moved about from one area to another, usually in search of food in different seasons.

Palaeontology The study of fossils and of ancient animals and plants.

Prehistoric Referring to anything that happened before recorded human history, about four thousand years ago.

Preserving The act of maintaining or keeping something in existence.

Reptile A class of animals that have scaly skins and lay eggs on land. Lizards and snakes are modern reptiles, as are crocodiles.

Rivals People who compete with one another for the same objective or in the same field of work.

Species A particular kind of animal or plant. Animals or plants of the same species can breed with one another and produce offspring.

Specimen An example of something.

Victorian The period of British history when Queen Victoria reigned (1837–1901).

Zoological To do with living animals.

Further Reading

Benton, Michael J. *Dinosaur Encyclopedia.* New York: Simon & Schuster Books for Young Readers, 1984.

Dingus, Lowell. *What Color Is that Dinosaur?* Brookfield, CT: Millbrook Press, 1994.

Dixon, Dougal. *Dougal Dixon's Dinosaurs.* Honesdale, PA: Boyds Mills Press, 1993.

Pearce, Q.L. *Tyrannosauraus Rex and Other Dinosaur Wonders.* Amazing Science. New York: Julian Messner, 1990.

Scheller, William. *Amazing Archaeologists and Their Finds.* Profiles. Minneapolis: Oliver Press, 1994.

Unwin, David. *Brachiosaurus.* Dinoworld. New York: Larousse Kingfisher Chambers, 1994.

The Dinosaur Society publishes a monthly newsletter called *DinoTimes* for young readers. To subscribe, write to: The Dinosaur Society, 200 Carleton Avenue, East Islip, NY, 11730, or call (516) 277-7855.

Museums

The American Museum of Natural History
Central Park West at 79th Street
New York, NY 10024
(212) 873-1300

The Brooklyn Museum
200 Eastern Parkway
Brooklyn, NY 11238
(718) 638-5000

The Field Museum of Natural History
Roosevelt Road at Lake Shore Drive
Chicago, IL 60605
(312) 922-9410

The Peabody Museum of Archaeology and Ethnology
Harvard University
Cambridge, MA
(617) 495 7535

The University Museum of Archaeology and Anthropology
University of Pennsylvania
33rd and Spruce Streets
Philadelphia, PA 19104
(215) 898-4000

Index